Tales of
Bunjitsu Bunny

Tales of Bunjitsu Bunny

Written and illustrated by
John Himmelman

SQUARE
FISH

Henry Holt and Company
New York

SQUARE
FISH

An Imprint of Macmillan
175 Fifth Avenue
New York, NY 10010
mackids.com

Square Fish and the Square Fish logo are trademarks of Macmillan and
are used by Henry Holt and Company, LLC under license from Macmillan.

Square Fish books may be purchased for business or promotional use. For information on bulk
purchases, please contact the Macmillan Corporate and Premium Sales Department at
(800) 221-7945 x5442 or by e-mail at specialmarkets@macmillan.com.

Library of Congress Cataloging-in-Publication Data
Himmelman, John, author, illustrator.
[Short stories. Selections]
Tales of Bunjitsu Bunny / written and illustrated by John Himmelman.
pages   cm
Summary: Although she can throw farther, kick higher, and hit harder than anyone else at
school, Isabel, aka Bunjitsu Bunny, never hurts another creature, unless she has to.
ISBN 978-1-250-06806-4 (paperback)   ISBN 978-0-8050-9972-0 (ebook)
[1. Martial arts—Fiction. 2. Rabbits—Fiction. 3. Animals—Fiction.] I. Title.
PZ7.H5686Taj 2014   [Fic]—dc23   2013048431

Originally published in the United States by Henry Holt and Company, LLC
First Square Fish Edition: 2015
Book designed by Ashley Halsey
Square Fish logo designed by Filomena Tuosto

10 9 8 7 6 5 4

AR: 3.1

*For my Hapkido and JKD family
at Green Hill Martial Arts*

Contents

Introducing Isabel   1

The Locked Door   3

The Pirates   10

The Race   20

The Challenge   28

Lucky Cricket   34

Splash!   43

Butterfly   52

Found   64

The Nightmare   71

The Wave   77

Bearjitsu Bear   88

The Rock   98

Interview with John Himmelman   121

Excerpt of Bunjitsu Bunny's Best Move   127

Introducing
Isabel

Isabel was the best bunjitsu artist in her school. She could kick higher than anyone. She could hit harder than anyone. She could throw her classmates farther than anyone.

Some were frightened of her. But Isabel never hurt another creature, unless she had to.

"Bunjitsu is not just about kicking, hitting, and throwing," she said. "It is about finding ways NOT to kick, hit, and throw."

They called her Bunjitsu Bunny.

The Locked Door

One afternoon, Isabel saw her
fellow bunjitsu students outside their
school. Teacher had left a sign on the
door. It read, "Come on in."

"Teacher wants us to go inside," said Max. "But the door is locked."

"It is a test," said Kyle. "He wants us to kick the door open." Kyle kicked the door as hard as he could.

"OW!" he yelped, hopping up and down on one leg.

"No," said Betsy. "He wants us to punch it down with our fists!" They all punched the door with their mighty bunjitsu fists.

"Ow! OW! OOCH! OWEE OWEE OWEE!" they said. The door hadn't moved an inch.

"I have an idea," said Ben.
"What's the hardest part of our
body?"

"The head," said Wendy.

"Right!" said Ben. "On the count of three, we will all perform the running bunjitsu head butt!"

"One . . . two . . ."

Suddenly, the door opened. Isabel
was on the other side. "Come on in,"
she said. "Teacher is waiting."

"How did you get in?" asked
Betsy.

Isabel pointed to the open
window by the door and said,
"When the door is locked, go
through a window."

The Pirates

Isabel loved to take her rowboat out on the pond. The warm sun felt good as her boat rocked gently on the water.

Suddenly, another boat bumped into her. Four mean-looking foxes stared at her.

"We are pirates," said one of
them. "Give us all your treasure!"

"I have no treasure," said Isabel.

"Then give us all your food!"

"I have no food," said Isabel.

"Then we will take you as our
prisoner."

The pirates grabbed Isabel and
pulled her into their boat.

"If you have nothing to give us,
we will throw you in the water,"
said a pirate.

Isabel grabbed the arm of the
nearest pirate and bunjitsu flipped
him over her shoulder. He landed
in her empty boat.

She then bunjitsu kicked the
second one so hard, he landed next
to his friend in her boat.

She threw the third pirate right on top of them.

The fourth pirate was so frightened, he crawled into her boat on his own.

"There," said Isabel. "Now you have my boat."

"We don't want your boat," said a pirate. "It is too small for us."

"Can pirates swim?" asked Isabel.

"Of course!" they said.

"Good," said Isabel. "Because your new boat is sinking."

Isabel sailed away. The warm sun felt good as her boat rocked gently on the water.

The Race

Sherman the tortoise loved to run, but he was always last in every race. No one wanted to race him because he was too easy to beat.

"I will race you to that tree across the field," said Isabel.

"You are Bunjitsu Bunny," said Sherman. "You will beat me very easily."

"Maybe, maybe not," said Isabel.

"On your mark. Get set. Go!"
Isabel shouted, and the race was on.

Isabel could have run right past
Sherman, but instead she stayed just
behind him.

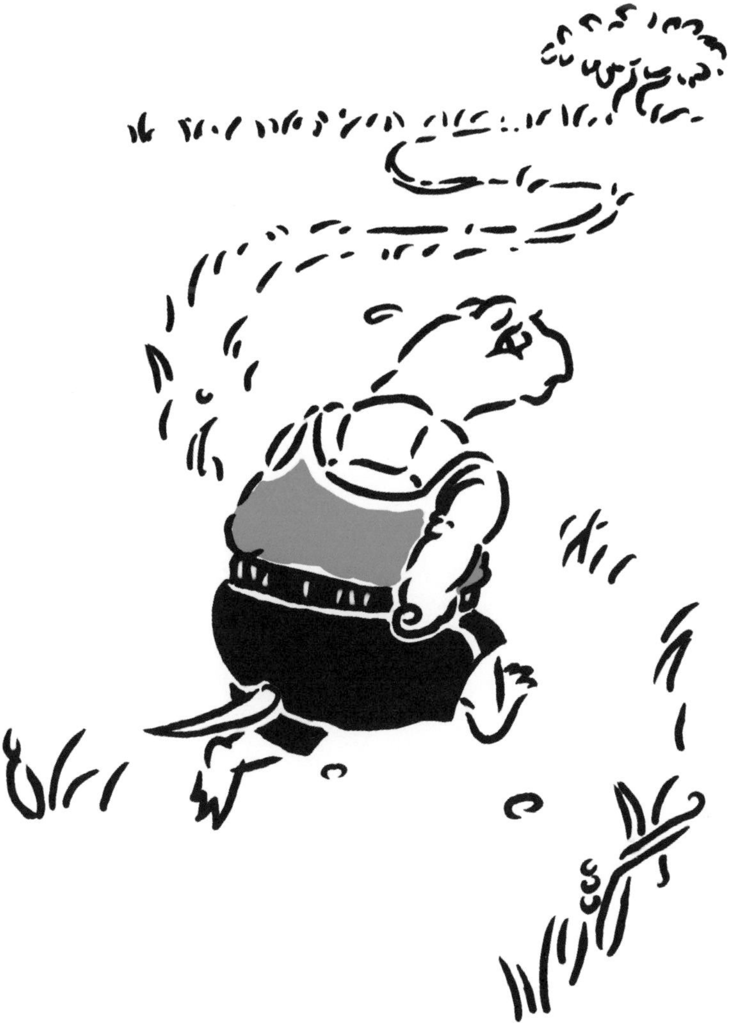

Sherman looked over his shoulder. *I am beating Bunjitsu Bunny,* he thought. He was so excited, he ran faster.

Isabel stayed right behind him. Whenever Sherman turned and looked, he saw she had almost caught him. This made him run even faster.

By the time he made it halfway to the tree, he was a blur of speed!

Sherman saw that Isabel was still right behind him. He gave it all he had. When he reached the tree, he was running so fast, he ran a whole extra mile before he could stop.

Finally, Isabel caught up.

"Did you let me win?" asked Sherman.

"I did at first," she said. "But as soon as you thought you could win, you won."

The Challenge

"I challenge Bunjitsu Bunny to a fight," announced Jackrabbit. "I will be waiting for her at the marsh in three days. I will hit her so hard, she will fly to the moon!"

Isabel's friends told her about Jackrabbit's challenge.

"He is so big," said Kyle. "Are you afraid?"

"I am not afraid of big things," said Isabel.

"He is so fast," said Wendy. "Are you afraid?"

"I am not afraid of fast things," said Isabel.

"He is so strong," said Ben. "Are you afraid?"

"I am not afraid of strong things," said Isabel.

Three days passed. Jackrabbit
was at the marsh. Everyone waited
for Isabel.

They waited.

They waited.

And they waited some more.

Finally, they got tired of waiting and went home. Even Jackrabbit lost interest and hopped out of the marsh.

Max found Isabel in the sandbox at the playground.

"Here you are!" he said. "Why didn't you go to the marsh?"

"He said he was going to hit me," said Isabel.

"So you lost on purpose?"

"No, I did not lose," said Isabel. "He did not hit me."

Lucky Cricket

Cricket chirped sweetly in the garden.

"Is it true that crickets bring good luck?" asked Isabel.

"Very true," said Cricket.

"I have a big bunjitsu tournament next week. Will you stay with me for luck?"

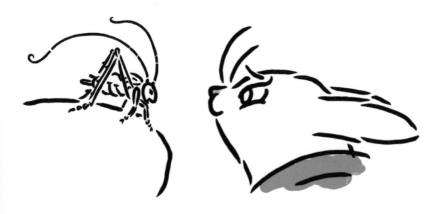

"Yes," said Cricket. "First, I need to see how much luck you will need. Show me your bunjitsu moves."

Isabel knew a LOT of bunjitsu moves, so it took her many hours to show Cricket.

The next day, Cricket said to
Isabel, "Could you show me those
moves again?"

She showed him
all of her kicks,
blocks, strikes,
and flips—
EVERYTHING
she knew.

When Isabel finished, Cricket said, "I'm sorry. I dozed off. Could you show me again?"

Isabel was very tired, but she did as Cricket asked.

For the next few days, Cricket asked Isabel to show him all her moves. She showed him over and over and over again. *Cricket sure is forgetful,* thought the bunny.

On the day of the tournament,
Cricket joined Isabel.

She won contest

after contest

after contest!

At the end of the day, Isabel said, "Thank you for bringing me luck, Cricket!"

"You were the one who practiced so hard every day," said Cricket. "I just let you make your own good luck."

Splash!

Isabel came upon her friends at the edge of a stream.

"Kyle kicked the ball across the water, and we need to get it back," said Betsy.

"I will get it," said Kyle.

First Kyle hopped onto a stump. Then he hopped onto the next stump. He tried to hop to the third stump. SPLASH! went Kyle into the water. He swam back.

"There's one way to get across this river," said Max. He grabbed a vine hanging from the trees. "EEEYYYAAAAA!" he shouted as he swung over the stream.

SPLASH! he went, as he fell in.

"I will try," said Betsy. She laid
a long stick across the stumps. She
balanced herself halfway across.

SPLASH! went Betsy into the
water. She swam back.

Isabel walked to the edge of the
stream and jumped in.

She climbed back out, grabbed
the vine, and swung over the water.

She dropped onto one of the
stumps. Hop, hop, hop she went,
across the stumps.

Then she walked across the stick
bridge to the other side.

Isabel picked up the ball and tiptoed over the stick bridge. A couple of hops and a swing later and she was back with her friends.

"Here is your ball," she said.

"You never needed to get wet,"
said Kyle.

"But once I did get wet," said
Isabel, "I didn't have to worry about
it anymore."

Butterfly

One day, Teacher said to his bunjitsu students, "I want you all to study an animal. In the next class, you will fight like that animal."

Isabel watched Butterfly in the meadow. "There are so many who want to eat you," she said. "And yet I see you in the meadow every day. Can you teach me what you do?"

"I would be honored to teach Bunjitsu Bunny," said Butterfly. "Try to catch me!"

Isabel tried to grab the slow-flying butterfly.

As soon as she got close, he quickly changed direction and flew away. She chased him all over the meadow. Whenever Isabel thought she had him, Butterfly surprised her with a burst of speed in a new direction.

The sun was going down, and it was time to go home.

"Thank you for teaching me," Isabel said to Butterfly.

The time came for the bunjitsu students to show what they learned.

Kyle studied a bear. He challenged Isabel.

Isabel strolled along the edge
of the mats. Kyle charged straight
at her. Isabel quickly changed
direction. Kyle could not catch her.

Wendy studied a cat. She
challenged Isabel. Isabel strolled
along the edge of the mats. Wendy
stalked her slowly . . . and pounced!
Isabel quickly changed direction.
Wendy could not catch her.

Betsy challenged Isabel. Betsy did
not say which animal she studied.
She and Isabel strolled along the
edge of the mats.

Whenever Betsy got close, Isabel quickly changed direction.

Whenever Isabel got close, Betsy quickly changed direction. This went on and on and on.

Finally Teacher said to the class, "Everyone might as well have a seat."

"Who is winning?" asked Kyle.

"There will be no winner," said Teacher. "Now let's all sit and enjoy the two butterflies in the meadow."

Found

Isabel and her friends liked to play hide-and-seek. Isabel was very good at hiding. She could make herself disappear behind anything. And sometimes she could hide even when there was nothing to hide behind!

"Isabel probably makes herself invisible," said her friends.

"Isabel just flies away," said her friends.

"Isabel shrinks down to the size of a bug," said her friends.

One afternoon, Isabel found
a great place to hide. Her friends
looked and looked for her. They
looked for hours, but they could not
find her.

Soon it was suppertime. They
all went home. Isabel did not know
they had stopped looking for her.
She began to get lonely. She missed
her friends. She jumped down from
her hiding place and walked home
alone. *That was not so much fun,*
she thought.

The next day, Isabel and her
friends played hide-and-seek again.
Betsy closed her eyes and counted
to ten while everyone hid. Isabel sat
down behind her.

"Eight . . . nine . . . ten," said
Betsy. She turned around and saw
Isabel sitting on the ground.
"I found you!" said Betsy.

Isabel stood up and shook her hand. "Good job," she said.

"Why did you make it so easy?" asked Betsy.

"It is more fun to be found by friends than lost by friends," said Isabel. And she and Betsy ran off to find the rest of their friends.

The Nightmare

One night Isabel had a scary
dream. In her dream, she was chased
by monsters. She woke up very
frightened.

The next night, Isabel was afraid to go to sleep. She stayed up all night, practicing her bunjitsu to stay awake. She was very tired in school the next morning.

Later that night, Isabel kept every
light on. She read books all night
long. She knew if she fell asleep, the
monsters would visit her.

When Isabel went to bunjitsu class the next day, Teacher asked, "Why do you seem so tired?"

"I can't sleep," said Isabel. "There are monsters in my dreams."

"Where do those dreams live?" asked Teacher.

Isabel pointed to her head. "In here," she said.

"Those monsters live inside the head of Bunjitsu Bunny?" he said. "I would be afraid to be THEM!"

Isabel smiled. Later that night, the monsters returned in her dream. This time they met with Bunjitsu Bunny. She sent those monsters away for good.

The Wave

"There is nothing more powerful than a wave," said Teacher. "If one can defeat an angry wave, one will be a true bunjitsu artist."

Isabel went to the beach. The waves were crashing on the shore.

She walked up to a wave and
gave it her best kick.

The angry wave picked her up
and tossed her back on the beach.

Isabel stood firm and put out her
hands to block the next wave.

The angry wave picked her up
and tossed her back on the beach.

Isabel gathered all the power in her lungs and shouted in her loudest voice, "STOP!"

The angry wave picked her up
and tossed her back on the beach.

Isabel was tired of being tossed
around. She was about to give
the next wave a spinning bunjitsu
tornado fist, but she stopped.

Instead, she sat down and let the
wave pick her up. She floated to the
top and rode it gently down to the
beach.

"This is so much more fun,
Wave," she said. "Thank you!"

The wave gave her ride after ride
until they both were tired.

The next day, Teacher asked, "Did you defeat the angry wave?"

"Yes," said Isabel. "It is no longer angry."

Bearjitsu Bear

Isabel was practicing her bunjitsu when Bear walked up to her.

"What are you doing?" he asked.

"It is called bunjitsu," said Isabel.

"Well, I practice *bearjitsu*," said Bear. "It is much better than your little bunny fighting."

"I am sure bearjitsu is good, too," said Isabel.

"What do you do in bunjitsu?" asked Bear.

"Well," said Isabel, "we kick pretty hard."

"Like this?" asked Bear. He kicked Isabel so hard she slid across the field.

"A little like that," said Isabel, dusting herself off.

"What else do you do?" asked Bear.

"We flip," said Isabel.

"Like this?" asked Bear. He grabbed Isabel's ears and flipped her to the ground.

"A little like that," said Isabel, straightening her ears.

"What else do you do?" asked Bear.

"We twist arms and legs," said Isabel.

"Like this?" asked Bear. He twisted Isabel into a pretzel.

"A little like that," said Isabel. "Please let go now."

"Do you give up?" asked Bear.

Isabel kicked Bear so hard he
shot straight into the clouds.

When he landed, she flipped him
to the ground so hard the earth
shook! Then she grabbed his giant
paw and twisted it behind his back.

"I give up!" shouted Bear.

"That's something I don't know how to do," said Isabel.

The Rock

One day, a big boulder rolled down the hill and landed in Isabel's yard.

"Oh no!" cried Isabel. "It crushed my flower garden." Isabel pushed and pushed the rock, but it would not move.

Then she found a large stick and rested it on a smaller rock. She pulled down as hard as she could to pry the big rock loose.

The stick broke. The rock did not move. Isabel's brother Max walked into the yard.

"Stand back!" he shouted. He ran
at the rock with a long stick.

The end of the stick struck the
rock. He pole-vaulted so far over it
that his sister lost sight of him.

"He'll find his way back in a few
hours," said Isabel.

Isabel looked down and saw a
little pink rock. She picked it up
and placed it next to the boulder.
It looked so pretty there. Then she
placed another smooth white rock
next to it.

Oh, how nice! she thought.

She placed a flat gray stone with the other rocks. Then she put a round one next to it.

Soon Isabel had covered the area with stones of all colors and shapes.

Max found his way back and
saw what she had done. "This looks
great!" he said.

"One rock is just one rock," said
Isabel. "Many rocks make a garden."

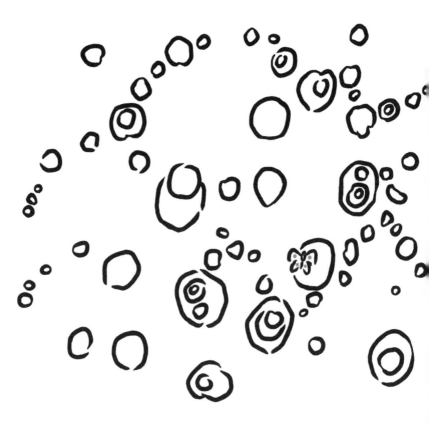

Later that night . . .

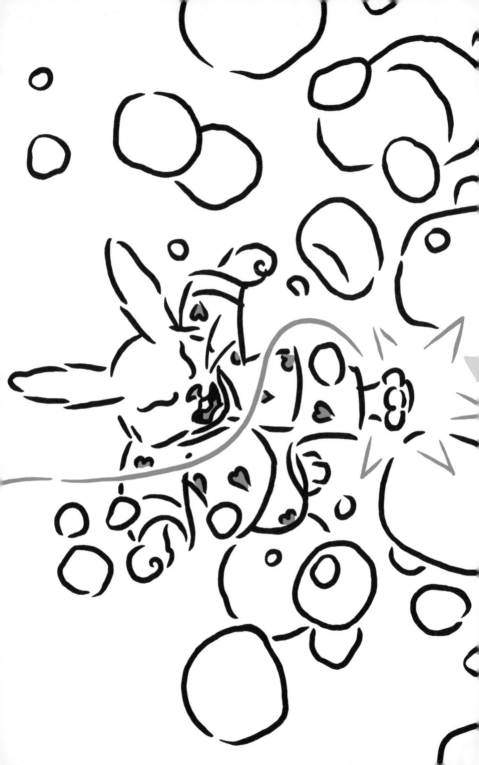

The Bunjitsu Code

All Bunjitsu students must do their best to follow the rules of Bunjitsu. If you wish to learn this art, you must read this and sign your name at the bottom.

I promise to:

- Practice my art until I am good at it. And then keep practicing.

- Never start a fight.

- Do all I can to avoid a fight.

- Help those who need me.

- Study the world.

- Learn from those who know more than I do.

- Share what I love.

- Find what makes me laugh, and laugh loudly. And often.

- Make someone smile every day.

- Keep my body strong and healthy.

- Try things that are hard for me to do.

GOFISH

JOHN HIMMELMAN

What did you want to be when you grew up?
In order from kindergarten to high school: scientist, entomologist, veterinarian, cartoonist.

When did you realize you wanted to be a writer?
I always enjoyed writing stories and drawing pictures. I honestly cannot think back on a time when I didn't!

What's your favorite childhood memory?
Playing outside with my friends and brothers on summer evenings. There was no school the next morning, so we'd stay out past dark—under the streetlights along our little dead-end road. It was such an exciting new world. Maybe that's why I enjoy exploring and writing about the nature found at night.

As a young person, who did you look up to most?
Besides my parents, my uncle Roland. He was a soldier who came to live with us when he returned from the Vietnam War. I have two younger brothers, but he was like an older brother to me.

What was your favorite thing about school?
Art class! It was always the highlight of my day. I was lucky to have very encouraging art teachers throughout my school years. And we got to listen to music during class.

What were your hobbies as a kid? What are your hobbies now?
I was really into bugs. I used to collect all different kinds and keep them in jars in my room. I'd study them for hours and hours, often drawing them. Now? I practice martial arts, play guitar, watch birds, chase butterflies, look for excuses to get together with friends, and . . . I collect all different kinds of bugs and keep them in jars in my room. I study them for hours and hours, often drawing them.

Did you play sports as a kid?
My dad would organize games for all the kids on our block. We played baseball, basketball, and football—depending on the season. I also played Little League baseball and CYO basketball.

What was your first job, and what was your "worst" job?
My first job was as a paperboy, delivering *Newsday* on my bicycle after school. It was also my worst job! I pedaled that overloaded bike through all kinds of weather every day of the week. Sundays were the worst! I had to get up at 5:00 a.m. to assemble the ad-bloated newspapers and then head out in two or three trips to deliver them. BUT, I made enough money to buy a new ten-speed bike and a camping tent!

What book is on your nightstand now?
There's never just one. *A Universe From Nothing* by Lawrence M. Krauss (I love space stuff), *Brave Companions: Portraits in History* by David McCullough (I love history stuff), and *Taijiquan: Through the Western Gate* by Rick Barrett (I love martial arts stuff). I'm also

hooked on The Walking Dead comics, but they get read too fast to make it to my nightstand.

How did you celebrate publishing your first book?
I had just graduated from college (School of Visual Arts), having had my first book (*Talester the Lizard*) accepted by a publisher. I bought a 1980 Subaru Brat and drove cross-country from my then-home in New York to California. The celebrations of books to follow never matched that first one.

Where do you write your books?
I sit at a big desk in my studio, surrounded by snoring dogs and a chirping cat. Just to my right is a big window to my garden, meadow, and wooded yard. It could be said that I spend too much time staring out that window, but I'd disagree.

What sparked your imagination for *Tales of Bunjitsu Bunny*?
When I opened my martial arts school (with fellow author Ed Ricciuti), a local paper did a story on us. The reporter featured one of our talented Hapkido students, eight-year-old Isabel. I shared the article with Kate Farrell, my editor at Holt, who then urged me to write a story about a girl who is an exceptional martial artist. I made the girl a bunny, created the art of "bunjitsu," and a world was born. The twelve tales in this and the next book, *Bunjitsu Bunny's Best Move*, are gleaned from lessons I have learned in martial arts and in life.

All the names of the characters in the book are or were students in our school. The signatures on the Bunjitsu Code in the back are the actual handwriting of each of those students!

Do you know how to do martial arts?
I practice and teach Hapkido and Jeet Kune Do at my school, Green Hill Martial Arts, in Killingworth, Connecticut. We recently moved

into a building built in 1881 that was once the town's meeting place for farmers, and then our old town hall. I love it there! I feel like we've become part of our town's long history!

What is your favorite thing about Isabel?
Isabel is very comfortable with who she is—so much so, she doesn't feel the need to prove her talents to others. But as skilled as she is, she's not perfect. She finds joy in conquering her challenges and learning new things.

What is more difficult for you: the writing process or the illustration process?
It depends on the book. The art for *Tales of Bunjitsu Bunny* is done in a looser style than I've used in the past. It is sometimes hard for me to say to myself, "STOP! Put down your brush! The picture is finished!"

What challenges do you face in the writing process, and how do you overcome them?
In the thirty-something years I've been doing this, I still don't know if what I write will be of interest to others. I keep telling myself it shouldn't matter, but if you make a living as a writer/illustrator, it kinda does. . . . I still try to write for myself, though, and just hope that afterward there will be someone out there who will enjoy reading it.

What is your favorite word?
Betsy. It's attached to my wife.

If you could live in any fictional world, what would it be?
I don't think there's a fictional world that can match the one I'm living in now.

Who is your favorite fictional character?
Gandalf the Grey.

What was your favorite book when you were a kid? Do you have a favorite book now?

The King With Six Friends by Jay Williams, illustrated by Imero Gobbato. My favorite book now is a picture book published in 1975, *Indian Bunny* by Ruth Bornstein. I guess I like rabbits? It's just so simple, so pure, and a little bit creepy.

If you could travel in time, where would you go and what would you do?

I sure would love to see some dinosaurs.

What's the best advice you have ever received about writing?

Fellow children's book author Kay Kudlinski always says, "Writers write!" So many people think about someday writing that story they always imagined they would write. Real writers don't think about it; they do it.

What advice do you wish someone had given you when you were younger?

"John, pay more attention in history class. You'll have less catching up to do when you realize there are no better stories than those of the people and events of our past."

Do you ever get writer's block? What do you do to get back on track?

I do. The best way to break through that wall is to write your way through it.

What do you want readers to remember about your books?

I want them to look at the faces in the pictures and know that as I was drawing every expression, I was wearing that same expression on my face. It's something I was told I do.

What would you do if you ever stopped writing?
I would find other ways to share stories, but writing is still the most comfortable way for me to do so.

If you were a superhero, what would your superpower be?
It comes down to the choice of being indestructible, invisible, or able to fly. Which would allow me the greatest advantage as a true force of good in this world? I tend to lean toward invisibility, but would not whine too loudly if either of the other two powers was bestowed upon me.

Do you have any strange or funny habits?
I sometimes pat my car and say "thank you" after getting home from a long trip. After years of doing this I found out that my grand-father used to do the same thing.

What do you consider to be your greatest accomplishment?
When asked this question, many people say their children. My son, Jeff, and daughter, Lizzie, however, are gifts, not accomplishments. So I'd say that finding a way to make a living that keeps me grow-ing and learning, that satisfies my unrelenting need to create is a pretty big accomplishment.

SQUARE FISH

Follow along with Isabel
on her next adventure.

Keep reading for a sneak peek of
Bunjitsu Bunny's Best Move.

Shadows

One day, Isabel and her brother,
Max, sat in a field. "Look at our
shadows on the rock," said Isabel.

"Let's see how well they know
bunjitsu," said Max. Max kicked his

foot in the air. His shadow kicked
its foot in the air. Isabel blocked the
kick. Isabel's shadow blocked the
kick.

"This is fun!" said Isabel.

Max's and Isabel's shadows
fought each other.

"My shadow has big teeth!" said
Max.

Isabel laughed. "My shadow has big antlers!" she said.

"My shadow has wings and can fly!" said Max.

"My shadow can tickle your shadow so it can't fly." Isabel laughed again.

Max moved away from the rock.
His shadow grew twice as large.
"Now you have to fight a giant
bear." Max's shadow pounded
Isabel's shadow with great big paws.
Isabel's shadow fell to the ground.

"My shadow has defeated the shadow of Bunjitsu Bunny!" said Max.

Isabel stood up and walked toward the rock.

"Now your shadow is like a little mouse," said Max.

"A quick little mouse," said Isabel.

Max's shadow tried to grab her shadow. Isabel's shadow darted away. Max's shadow tried to punch Isabel's shadow. Isabel's shadow darted away. Her little shadow was too quick for Max's shadow.

"I give up," said Max. "I thought being bigger and stronger would make me win."

"Sometimes," said Isabel. "But sometimes it's better to be a little mouse than a great big bear."